EREBIAN MUSINGS

Erebian Musings

Leigh Koonce

Ellerslie Books

My Thanks To...

Dr. Alan Tinkler, who fostered my desire to write and kickstarted it from a private, guilty pleasure to something I relished sharing with others.

Brenda, Eric, Ron, Debbie, and Kendra who have all managed or owned bookstores in which I've "worked" over the years, thus fueling my book buying addiction.

Barnes and Chelf, who may not remember it, but ready many of the pieces in this collection and didn't punch me in the face with scorn.

My muse, Jessica Fletcher. I've got the writing part down, now it's time to start solving murders in rural Maine and beyond.

Contents

Chapters from "It's Just a Life," an unfinished novel

Definitions

erebian adj. /AIR-eh-bee-an/ dark or having to do with darkness. Derived from Erebus, the personification of darkness in Greek mythology.

musings noun /MU-zings/ newspaper columns written by three-time Substitute Teacher of the Year, Mrs. Hank "Peggy Platter" Hill.

Introduction

To my dear friends (and hopefully new friends who don't know me, but have purchased this book), I offer up this collection of little short stories, prose poetry, an essay, and some chapters from a book I never finished for your kind review.

The first question you may have is WTF's with the title. Well, who doesn't love Erebus, the Greek mythological personification of darkness? Oh, just me? No really, I coined this new word "erebian" because, believe it or not, every single one of these stories was written at night. I can't explain it, but I'm rarely struck with a creative spark while the sun is out. Even when I was writing academically or professionally as a journalist or copywriter, night time was the key. And the musings. Well, again, who doesn't love a good *King of the Hill* reference? Plus, these are simply that, musings. I've only submitted three for publication and, frankly, didn't think they were good enough to put out into the sphere of creative writing. But, after some thought, I decided, why not?

Thanks for reading!

Laters,

Leigh Koonce

1

I Promise I Never Had a Guitar in High School

It's true, I promise. I never had, played, or even looked at a guitar in high school. I've never been musically inclined, but I bring up the guitar as an example. Unless I'm totally off center, a fair majority of us had a pseudo-hobby in high school that's pretty popular among teenagers. And unless I'm wrong again, most of us weren't terribly good at whatever hobby it was. Maybe we didn't share our interest (however strong it may have been) with many people out of fear of being totally cringe and untalented. Of course I suppose many of us thought we were legends and quite overtly displayed and discussed our talent, or lack thereof.

First, at what was I total crap? Most things, but between the time I was 14 and 20 (or so), I explored several hobbies, including soccer (miserable), skateboarding (several sprained wrists), and tennis (passable, but I'm not big on being in the sun). Let's take them in turn and remember, it took me three sets of lessons over the course of two years to learn to swim.

Soccer, aka football everywhere else, was of interest mainly after watching the World Cup. I never played it as a kid, but I was interested enough as a teenager to order a ball off the internet, and kick it around in my backyard, which kind of drove my dog crazy. I tried to play keep ups a lot, but wasn't great. Clearly, the problem was I didn't have the right gear, so I ordered a couple of England jerseys and some bright shoes in various colors. Turns out it wasn't the lack of gear, I just truly was untalented in that pursuit.

Let's skip ahead to tennis, which was one of those things my Mom thought it was imperative that I learn to do to be "well-rounded." So, she signed me up for tennis lessons at a public park. I was probably 12, maybe 11, but all I remember is being in the sun with a ton of kids ranging in age from possibly 10 to 15 and trying to bounce a ball on the racket. One day was enough for me and I promptly informed my Mom I'd lock myself in my room and "never come out" if I was to go back. Even though that one experience wasn't great, I didn't totally close the door on tennis. My Mom enjoyed watching Wimbledon and just from being in the same house, I happened to watch it from time to time, also. So, much like the soccer experiment, I took to banging around some tennis balls in my backyard and played, casually, with some friends. It's safe to say serving certainly wasn't my strong suit.

Back to skateboarding. Perhaps the most complicated relationship I have with a casual hobby is with skateboarding. We had maybe two skaters in my entire school, so it wasn't a very popular pursuit at that time where I was. I'm not sure how I ever got the idea that I wanted a skateboard but thanks to my parents' credit card and the internet, one is featured in my inventory of online purchases. Of the three aforementioned pursuits, this is the one I took the most seriously. I read *Thraser* magazine, watched online videos, and practiced in the driveway. While I was interested and it was kind of fun, I never gave it the dedication needed to become anything more than a really poor amateur.

I've never totally closed the door on skateboarding though, and as I write this one of my boards sits in my parents' dining room under the table for no reason other than that's where I last dropped it. I dug it out of the basement over the summer on a whim. It landed in the basement two years ago, because I had the third of the three fairly minor injuries I experienced over the years thanks to skateboarding.

At least I never had a guitar, though.

2

James Franco Offers My Orange Vomit

A parade of writers force me to put pen to paper. Sitting at the desk and staring out the window forces them into view. Green liquid down the throat insists I'm not crazy. A foggy figure drifts into the library.

Virginia Woolf holds out a dripping hand. I refuse to take it and she throws a wet stone at my head. I suspect she bought them herself. Grasping the ungraspable hand transports me to the lighthouse. Screeching seagulls and crashing waves. Relaxing? Yes. Traumatic? No. She invites me to swim with her. I refuse.

James Franco emerges from the lighthouse door and we are suddenly in Palo Alto, dodging an out-of-control Mustang driven by a drunken teenager. Thankfully we aren't real. Wait a minute, why then am I bleeding from the stinging scrape on my knee? I see a pineapple roll down the street. He watches it before projectile vomiting an orange mélange of chunky liquid onto my Toms. Muttering a shaky "Dude," he scoops some up with a hand and offers it to me. "Swallow this and you'll write like me." Decisions. I could always take it and try it later. Probably best if I pass, though. The only orange thing I own is a bicycle.

I turn away to see a dirty street in Dublin. James Joyce exits a whore house and gestures at me with his cane. I squish over to him and accept an envelope from his hand. A stamp is affixed to the corner and a shaky pen has written Nora's address in black, slightly smudged ink. Without thinking I begin to open the envelope but stop as Joyce's cane connects with my hand. He shakes his finger at me and I sheepishly walk half a block (around horse-shit) to drop the communication into a pillar box. I turn to see JJ tip his hat to me and then walk back into the temple of the night.

A late model 40s sedan pulls up to the curb, brakes squealing and I get in. Soon, with Neal Cassady behind the wheel and Jack Kerouac sitting next to him, we're speeding down a nondescript, endless stretch of highway. Neal is sweating from the Benzedrine, presumably, even though all of the windows are open. Jack O'Lantern wraps his scarf tightly around his neck and scribbles away with a desiccated pencil. I drink from the warm cans of PBR Jack passes around and swallow the pills Neal digs out of his shirt pocket. Fucked out of my mind, I drift off despite the bumpy road and hair-pin turns.

The pen is moving without my instruction. Before I open my eyes, I hear a falcon screech. Open. An Edwardian library, a very dapper W.B. Yeats standing beside a miniature cyclone under glass. Automatic writing. Of course. Looking down I see a grocery list: raisins, rice, gin, cucumbers, taco shells, and purple-monkey-dishwasher. Yeats takes the paper, reads, shakes his head, and throws it into the fireplace.

A giant trunk falls from the ceiling and as the lid opens Thomas de Quincey climbs out. I'm back in my room with the glass still half full of green. Pen in hand. de Quincey reaches out and adds a drop of red from his flask. He pulls handkerchief out of his pocket and wipes his damp brow. I pick up the glass and watch it dilute. One sip--I'm off on another trip.

3

If Skrillex Used More Words in His Songs

Skrillex gives the listener an acid trip for the ears, sometimes the mind, and never flashbacks. The mind orgasms when *Made in Chelsea*, James Joyce, and Skrillex mix into one giant ball of melted brilliance topped with juxtaposed Queen's English and bound with string of ethereal evanescence.

If Skrillex used more words in his songs and I listened while reading Jimmy Joyce or watching *MIC* my brain might liquefy and slowly drip out of my ears and nose, saving the Egyptian hook-masters some time. Possibly spoiling their fun, though.

Perhaps these ancient undertakers can explain contemporary pop culture references to me? Mentioning a Jeopardy clue from last night is about as vapid as I can sound without being disingenuous. The more words I use the less realistic I become.

My hair used to be a bird's nest. It does take some effort to look that gross. Just ask me about that time I had to cut the knots out with scissors and found pine needles. If I hadn't cut it, I'd now have dirty dreadlocks, but traveling religions would leave me alone.

I like to paint pictures with oil paints. I have no talent so they only look like the mind of a psychopath on shrooms. Lacking talent can be good—most pop culture figures—for one's pocketbook. Or bad—me—which leads to a spill on the floor, size 13 sneaker prints, and a bill for a new Persian rug.

Want to read James Joyce? Walk Dublin for 5 years, read a stack of books about Irish history, and then start with *The Dubliners*. Coward.

It's simple.

If Skrillex used more words in his songs he'd be James Joyce.

4

Gilligan's Island Brought Me to a New School

Blue pigs tried to help by chasing me onto a shoe shine chair. Elevated above the grime ridden tile floor to which I fell before all was done, dizzy as if climbing the Alps. Wind up monkey chilly in the night air. Can't forget him. Did my newspaper swaddling help?

Little philosopher's unspeakable act drowns out imitation sirens and blinds more than glaring red lipstick. All alone left in one piece unwanted. Repeated glances of silence through venetian blinds. Unable to speak save through bloodless money—all that's left in California.

Young lady of the night danced with lonely streetlights at 1 am. Collected like trading stamps for being an unsubstantiated tr---. Oedipal knowledge useless. Natural growth and maturity sealed off the lifeline. Rebelling without a cause in the vain attempt to return to normalcy while knowing the new normal can never be like the old normal which is no longer normal but rather alien, startling, bipolar. Lonely.

Bruised and cut knuckles gracing vein-filled hands resulting from wooden boxing match. Grey shadow of stability offering assistance falls short. Just enough too late? Cones of liquid cooled situational rage brought on by wishy washy vacillation exhibited with greater ease than through an invertebrate.

Little philosopher shivers but refuses an offer of warmth, wrapping himself in icy rejection repeated three hundred times. Future friend with the most tragic story to tell and heartbreaking soul crushing end. A tectonic shift on the anniversary of birth. A flicker of happiness destined to be snuffed out.

Young lady of the night waits expectantly. A glimmer of hope known to be lacking in reality. Distinguished graying head of house doesn't arrive. Betrayal. Juvenile longing intensified by apron strings longing trying to form a net of safety.

Country club speeches delivered from a tuxedo while worrying what neighbors will say. Tearing soft skin sinewy muscle hard bone as if composition paper. Pecked by hens at every turn until no armor remains. Humming a hundred tunes while hunched over distracts from concrete jungle absurdity.

Three best friends/strangers leave separately, unaware of numbers and ranks.

Stinking of alcohol and cologne--grown up smells emanating from a teenager trapped in brown blazer straightjacket. Juxtaposition junction. Hard muscle stubble free chin. Rampant sex drive virgin body. Worldly desires immaturity. Walking contradiction with mop of curly hair. The rest of life begins tomorrow with the termination of innocence.

5

Beats

1947 newspaper, November 12th exactly, resting under unbroken beer bottles, full ashtrays, not yet moldy coffee cups with crust of bread from a cheese sandwich. Picking it up presupposes unsetting the table, possibly organizing scattered words. Dadaist experimentation improved upon with syringes, leaving behind razor blades until 1993.

A too gaunt arm eventually becoming yellowishly tarplike still balances the dull pencil hovering over sheets of typewriter paper rendered 50% useless by lack of fresh ribbon inserted into the mechanized raindrops on tin rooves captured by countless bleach blondes in mohair sweaters worn to the expansive uptown pools which run dry 365 out of 365 plus 1 every quarter of 16. Angular letters match square stubble ridden jaw which remains thusly in 4 hours when found in the integrated jazz hall thick with music permeating clouds of loud smoke.

The X-convict carrying the psychoanalyzed-to-the-point-of-exhaustion-kid flies around the fog as an antithesis of the zeppelin, emerging as the very thesis of the movement. His system somehow vulcanized beyond human perception offers a Platonic tonic which no one can replicate.

Entering with an ever-present cloud eviscerated of liquid rain is the imperfect rebirth of Stoicism prone to using muscled fists in the face of both destiny and disposition. Sun colored face remains expressionless while shouldering past drunken sailors to the best Cabaret Voltaire booth west or east of the Matterhorn.

Upon seeing his sometime twin across the room the sorest of thumb's orbit pulls along the son-of-a-mental-patient and the gang is all here sans a forgotten master of arts channeling an earth-shattering movement who will always be, like Latin, forgotten but by the dustiest of niche hipsters overflowing with pretention and hard-ons for anti-Communist spewing non-academic bisexual pseudo-scholars. Go!

Conversation gushes forth from two ejaculating mouths, forced into slower streams through narrow tunnels by four ears. Gide and Emily D wind up in Walden furiously fucking the glassiest of hearts living deliberately in 1815. Rolling the results into a joint, served with a side of Benzedrine greases the works causing explosive fireworks of creativity serving to pay homage to the new Earth's pantheon of greats.

Designed sleepless nights remembered by inflated word counts added to empty bottles and divided by heart rate jolting cups of coffee cement the unnatural bond of four disparate travelers. Four disparate travelers, take 3 or give 9, juxtaposing a fear of idealist normalcy with rampant desire for exploration and traveling the totem of taboos vilified by black robes.

Learned experience croaks forth from the slight, bushy haired youngster. Simplicity silences the flow of sexual escapades, stolen cars, grandiose theories. Unnatural that became natural is replaced with an appreciation of nature. So it begins.

6

Friends Come In and Out of Your Life Like Busboys

Apparently the above noted quotation is from a film called *Stand By Me*. I've never seen it, but am vaguely familiar with the film because of an episode of *The Simpsons*.

The quotation came to my attention through a recently purchased graphic novelization of *Riverdale*, a comic book series based upon the CW television show based upon the comic book juggernaut *Archie*. Basically, the traditional characters are updated and put into situations more akin to a mélange of *Broadchurch* and *The OC*. The important part, though, is the application of the quotation to one's personal life.

On the face of it, the underlying meaning is very dower and rather heartbreaking. As one navigates the alleys of life, from elementary school to high school to university, and then, presumably, the workforce, a certain number of relationships are bound to crop up.

In elementary school, I had several friends with whom I was close. As a naïve eight or nine year old, I, as many do, assumed those childhood friendships would be forever lasting. Of course they weren't. Parents move, children change schools, interests diverge. Middle school wasn't much different. The revelation came for me, at least, once I hit high school.

As a teenager, I wound up, partially at my request, at a small Catholic preparatory school where I was originally to know zero of my roughly 250 classmates. Fate swooped in and brought along one person I knew, a former classmate from preschool, as well as part of elementary and middle schools.

So there I was, a petulant, typically bored and shy new kid surrounded by lots of people who had been in school together their entire lives. (Not to mention the fact I was in another state and about an hour from home for a third of the day.) I won't dramatize it—there were a lot of students who came in that year from West Virginia and who didn't know many other people, too.

While it did take me a while to adjust, I immediately knew the setting was right for me. Small class sizes, challenging and intellectually based work, and people with whom I shared commonalities. The first year was still a learning experience, but by the second year I quickly realized I had hit a stride which wasn't totally uncomfortable or soul crushing (all right, I'll be slightly dramatic).

I became friends with a small group of people, but since the school was about one fifth the size of most schools, I felt as though everyone knew everyone else in our class, if not those above and below as well. Our yearly retreats, during which time we were essentially shipped off to a one star hotel for a few days of bonding exercises, succeeded in bringing us all closer together, even if only in agreement that the accommodations were well below standard.

Due to the small size of the school, it was quite common to have multiple classes with the same people each year. Add to that the small lunchroom, the segregation by year at mass, study groups, extracurriculars, and carpools and it was nearly impossible not to develop some strong friendships. So, does high school really prove this classic movie quotation wrong? We'll return to this question in a page or two.

After I graduated, I became wrapped up in politics, did some traveling, took an internship at a law office, and pretty much didn't "look back." I suppose those actions made me the aforementioned busboy. I started up some new friendships, rekindled others from elementary school, and maintained a quite busy schedule which didn't permit for as much socializing as I'd enjoyed a year earlier. It didn't take more than two seasons before I started busing those old tables again, but a new problem presented itself. College.

My original hope had been to study abroad. I was accepted at two schools in England, but I knew I wanted to take a year off. During that time my Dad developed a perforated ulcer and nearly died. Further, I became even more involved in local politics and thus decided I wanted to stay put. Some of my friends from high school made the same decision and were close at hand.

Others went away and emails, messaging, and the like assisted with communication.

While I opted to attend a fairly small college, it still had approximately 25 times the number of students as my high school. So, massive in my eyes. That didn't stop me from meeting people and forging new friendships. I even bumped into people from my old elementary school and high school from time to time. Something was missing though.

The first few semesters I don't recall being in the same class with the same person more than once in a given semester. Couple that with the fact that most classes were three times a week, sometimes only once a week, and it was difficult to establish the same meaningful relationships with people. Perhaps this led me to fortify those friendships from high school and continue to focus on them.

To forge on, though, a breaking point did occur and I made several new friends in literature courses, which I idealistically thought would last forever. I was much of the same mind as the eight year old me who thought a mutual love of Zelda videogames and Power Rangers would be the cement to hold a friendship together for 80 years. Of course, I was naïve.

There always seem to be things that crop up which cause one to see less and less of friends. Work, geography, new people. The frequency of hanging out lessens. The encyclopedic knowledge of one's friends becomes a much shorter volume as mundane life events are no longer shared on a regular basis. Sometimes it's one sided; not for want of trying on the part of one person does the friendship fizzle out. Other times people just drift apart.

I shouldn't be too harsh, though, as some of these literature class friendships have remained and are, at least from my standpoint, still flourishing today, which brings us directly to the exercise portion of this essay. Is this lofty minded quotation, presented in quite boiled down language, apt?

Short answer: yes.

Long answer: yes, but…

I think chance plays a large part in the length of friendships. While carefully analyzing a selection of friendships over the years, there are some people with whom I remain quite close, but with whom I share little in common. Of course interests change over the years; I used to be super-fascinated with the Modernist literature movement, but now favor the Medieval period. Further, my interest in soccer and *Eastenders* has given way to a focus on 1970s cop shows and abstract painting. Logically, then, friendships can be lost when interests evolve and the commonalities once shared are no longer present.

I will be remiss to not discuss geography in this context. For all the times people in the universe have uttered "Dude, it doesn't matter how far away we live from one another, we'll still be mates," or some variant, it actually does matter in most cases. I can say with complete certainty that living within visiting proximity of someone definitely makes it easier to maintain a close friendship. Some of my friends from high school live states away and while we're still friends, the ferocity of the friendship has waned over the years. Just to be contrarian though, one of my oldest friends lives about 15 minutes away from me and we're lucky if we get together once a year.

The final point, yes almost to the end, is to touch upon fast friendships, as I'll call them. I'm referring to a friendship that starts normally but which finds one hanging out or communicating with that same person to a herculean degree in a short amount of time. Whirlwind friendships seem to happen a lot at school. Stupid dumb group work is assigned and one gets partnered up with a fellow student, with whom a great deal of time is spent in a short time.

What's my conclusion? I must admit I've been pretty lucky to maintain friendships from various arenas and from the different phases of my life. However, there are those people with whom I was friends who I haven't spoken with in quite a while or see far less frequently and that is cause for some degree of sadness.

Vice, *GQ*, and other magazines are constantly running articles detailing specific times when people find themselves mostly friendless or adrift from even their closest friends. Various reasons are given—romantic relationships, moving, work—but the bottom line is that the loss of a friend is something through which everyone must go.

I'm a very nostalgic person and often find myself reminiscing about past events, which often leads me to wonder "what ever happened to" this person or that person—those with whom I've lost contact. It's typically impossible to recreate events, which includes social events. Thus, while it may have been fun when a group of us went to a specific museum or shopping center, it is never possible, with or without those same people, to recreate that exact outing. I suppose whilst friends are busboys, memories are that really bad bout of food poisoning that one never forgets having contracted with a specific restaurant, but it a really good way.

7

Giant Ladybug Number Three

Creaky floor vibrating with loud music and sound of liquid. Steam rises and tickles the yellow bananas strung up by the stems. Stinging, slow, sandy eyes glimpse dark closet serving as storage for broom and telephone. Saucers, bags, mason jars, buckets full of merchandise serving to allay fears of generic substitutes being parlayed to the slow-witted and suspicious.

Line of aging hippies, pretentious middle-classers, and young hipsters forms crookedly beside Nixon's resignation. Open door invites the breeze of cigarette smoke and street noise. Barking questions and thanks burst forth from the cell sized work area. Cash only goes into the till as yoga mom departs, followed by Prius-driving, retired something or another.

Dread-locks with sketchbook and bicycle girl dodge patriotism as they seek a stimulant. A wet dog passes quickly, providing a brief glimpse of orange and white. I beg a cup filled with blooms of white roses and peonies, promising to bring Alexander Hamilton tomorrow.

Assurances follow in retreat past books and peace signs. Bar Kitty's pedestal draped in flowers, grime, and a black light's wet dream awaits next to the king and queen and their court. Eyeballs on the wall silently judge as Forlinghetti is dissected for curious exploration next to the odor-filled Facebook check-in. Albert Hofmann painted the ceiling and fell into the walls, exploding into 1,936 pieces. 1,937 on Ash Wednesday.

A howl from behind jars of specimens and I leap to my feet, avoiding lava with the aid of giant ladybug number three. Steaming red is placed into hand, radiating pain to the brain. Tongue is burned but sand is washed away from eyes. Fleeing provides cool breeze on face, followed up by slap of Americanism. I press on, down stairs and off toward the clock, loud mess a.k.a. paradise--lost.

For the moment.

8

Andrew Wyatt Stole My Hair

Lighthouse lamp illuminating the room to enable Andrew Wyatt-hair to be cut. Say good-bye to an old friend. Lava lamp-tears at the *Finnegan's Wake* held for long hair. Scissors on the floor next to *Loaded,* Kerouac, and aborted projects. No afterbirth, regrettably. The ceiling holds nothing save a vent; orifice to the nerve center. Dusty curtains never used as capes to jump from the roof to superhero flight or certain broken leg.

Interruption due to electricity through the brain, the constant reminder of craziness. Creative craziness that leads to brilliance or disaster. Depends on the day. Pink to stop the vibrations.

Closet monsters with jagged teeth, coiling tails, blood under nails kept at bay by a coat hanger across the knobs. Check every night. Every night to make sure it's empty; devoid of untouchables. Two doors, like eyes that see all. Long hair gone, pain.

Pink, sleepiness. Reading, happiness. Eating. Masturbation. Sex. Nudity. Embarrassing. Love for the flag. god save the Queen.

Butcher knife under the pallet. Just in case. Dull blade, vertically not horizontally. Within reach should the FOOTPAD crest the stair and seek blood with cufflinks, money, and documents. The carpet hasn't been scotch guarded.

Pink yogurt stain. July night. Panic through the arm. Too hot. Breathing shallow, dizzy; why? So hot, sweating. Cancer! TB! The Plague! All the illnesses. Crazy. Cherry with a spoon fell off the table.

Desk of dreams. Words, pens, wax, skull bank, *New Yorker*. Royal velvet, straight-back chair. Uncomfortable. Royal we shall receive one at our earliest opportunity. Locked drawer with passport, stamped to heaven (England) and hell (America). Empty red soda can, sand and cigarette ends within.

Craziness held at bay by silent sentinels, James Dean clock and framed George McGovern. We shall sleep now.

9

Abortion Alley

I always feel as though my dress shoe clad feet project a rather hollow, haunting sound on stone sidewalks. Something akin to an executioner's slow, deliberate march to the cell of the damned, or perhaps the footfalls of a stalking serial killer, meandering around the streets, seeking his next victim.

It's cold tonight. My breath escapes my mouth in pale clouds. The stark moon stares down at me from a sky devoid of an entourage of clouds. I'm waiting in a dark alley; Abortion Alley, as it has been called. About a year ago a friend sent me a photo in a text message of a coat hanger, rusty, on the ground in this alley. Nothing more than a joke. A light socket hangs over a doorway which leads into a shop, but the bulb is either dead or missing. The opposite street is visible as some light pours out of a shop window, illuminated so that those passing by can bear witness to the antiquated fashion designs of a second hand paradise. For lack of anything better to do my hands drift to the collar of my coat and pull it up around my neck. The scarf, already tight like a noose, is keeping most of the cold air from my throat.

I can hear a voice raised in the distance, presumably coming from the entrance way to a bar which rests across the street and to the left. I hear it again. A car drives by, its windows up, but the radio is loud enough that I hear a deep bass line. My senses are on high alert. I know I shouldn't be here, shouldn't be doing this. I don't fight in the trenches; I plan from the safety of the rear ranks.

The giant bell in the heavenly-high clock tower begins to strike eleven, sending long, low echoes to the mortals below. The sound of gravel crunching under heavy feet emanates from behind me. A tall, broad shouldered figure begins to climb the five stone steps which lead into Abortion Alley. The building to his left is a restaurant, and the pipes from some contraption in the kitchen are blowing steam or exhaust, or something out, which swirls around his silhouette, and gives the appearance of a scene from a B-movie thriller. He stops a few feet from me.

My mouth is dry.

"Are you Jake's friend?" The voice has an educated air about it with strong diction.

"What if I am?" Admittedly not the best answer; well, not even close.

"Whether you are or not, it makes little difference to me." He begins to walk past me.

"No, wait! I am." We were almost face to face now. He stands a bit taller than my six feet, is clean shaven, and has unruly hair.

"Pleased to meet you then. I'm Ren. Warren really, but I don't care for the full name." He holds out his hand and I shake it firmly.

When he releases his grip and pulls back, the $100 bill I had pressed into his hand falls to the ground.

He looks slightly puzzled as I lean down and scoop up the money in a frantic panic.

"You're supposed to put it in your pocket," I hiss. "What if someone saw?"

"Saw you acting like a half-crazed jackass?" he replies. "This isn't a street corner in downtown New York."

"There are cops in this town."

"Yes. Two at this time of night." He reaches into his coat pocket and produces a small plastic bag with a host of small white pills in it.

Ren thrusts the bag at me. "Take it."

"Keep your voice down." I snatch the bag from him and put it in the interior pocket of my coat. I covertly held out the money.

"It's not heroin, you know. There's no need to be so scared."

I brush imaginary dust from the sleeve of my coat. "I'm not accustomed to this type of thing."

"What's the difference between buying a few Denzo pills from me or going to the pharmacy, aside from the ambiance of course?" Ren took up a slouching stance against the wall.

I came to realize that I was shifting from one foot to another. "The major difference is the whole illegality nonsense of meeting a stranger in a dark alleyway and paying three times the normal price for a plastic bag of pills I only hope won't kill me."

"Small wonder you're buying what you're buying. Anyway, I'd better be off. You know how to reach me when you need more. Good night." Ren nodded his head as he turned and walked off back the way he had come.

I drove home as carefully as I could in the hopes that I wouldn't be stopped for some minor traffic infraction by an over-zealous police officer, who would then feel the need to search my person and find a plastic bag full of pills. Getting out of the car I can feel the dizziness that has been plaguing me for days. Even with the frigid temperatures, my brow is damp with sweat.

The bark of a fox sounds from the woods and I exhale a slight gasp, taken by surprise. Going this long only makes the anxiety worse, as if some unknown hand is doling out extra (or fewer) chemicals in my brain, attempting to unleash an electrical pulse filled masterpiece while throwing the whole balance to hell.

I was okay during my exchange with Ren, probably because that was at the forefront of my mind, not my impending death by any number of ridiculous means.

As I hurry inside and into the kitchen, I leave behind a trail. Scarf. Coat. Shoes. Sweater. One of the perks of living alone, perhaps? Fiji water from the fridge and bag in hand, the ascension of the stairs is next. I pass photographs and paintings of my family from many generations. Silent reminders of stronger folks.

I flip the light on, turn up Miike Snow, and down three pills with water. As I flop down on my bed I can already feel the dizziness slipping away. The numbness is refreshing.

10

Walls

Dripping like the wall is melting. Lava, hot wax, scalding oil running down the drywall. Mixing. Mixing. Everything is mixing. Blood with paint. Ink and egg yolks. Semen joining molten earth. I don't want to be burned. I can't stop my hand from moving. It's strangling me. Stopping. Crawling on my face like a spider, stepping into my eyes, tripping in my hair. I restrain it. Restrain myself. Stop!

The boiling liquid is almost upon me. Not tea. God save the Queen, anyway. I jump onto the blue bubble. My foot's caught between the cushions. The purple lava turns into a green rhino, charging the blue bubble. Pull. Pull. My leg's free and so am I. For a split second. Weightless, floating. Gravity rapes me and pulls me down. Smash onto the floor. Crash. Rash. From the heat? Where's the melted wall?

Stand up. Metal in my mouth. A spoon? Bullets? Change? Metal. Metal. Drink the floor. Stop the taste. Burn my mouth. The floor is dry. Where did it go? The rhino. He drank it all; turned himself into a blue elephant. Grew.

Peanuts. I need peanuts so the elephant will give me a drink. Shower me with cold water from his trunk. Bathroom shower. Shells in the drain. Water flooding. Not yet. Peanuts. Where are the peanuts? Peanuts. Peanuts. Peanuts. Peanuts. Peanuts. Peanuts.

"Butler. Bring the elephant peanuts!"

Silence.

"Butler! Peanuts!"

I'm alone. Just my elephant and I. The walls dried up. The floor is parched. Cracks. Opening. Metal in my mouth. Coins. I'll pay the butler with my tongue, but I have no butler.

Sink. I can find a sink. I'll open a hole in the wall. Its forcefield will open out like a book cover. James Joyce. Edgar Allan Poe. They'd be my friends. Jane Austen is gross. Pull. The hole opens. It has spots. Purple spots. Red spots. Dots. Dots of yellow. Yellow and red join. I hide my eyes. Embarrassed. Pop! They're orange. Dots are darting around. Spots are spilling down the stairs. Mop. I need a mop.

"Butler! Mop up the spots."

The wall is shedding. Skin falling off. Blue skin. Blue blood. Aristocrat. That's me. I run to save the wall. Footsteps. Mine. Sound, mini-earthquakes. Sound waves. Discs. Records. Blue skin. Ice cold. Too cold. Burning cold. The elephant. He's blue. Frozen? Pluto.

Run to save him. The hole's corked. Help! Sewn closed. How can I save him? Pull. Pull. Push? Fall forward. Down. Over. He's gone. Missing. 5. 4. 8. 3. No phone. S.O.S. Morse. Inspector? Code.

Alone.

The walls are spreading. The room is huge. Football field. Library of Congress. Giant. Universe. No walls. No elephant. I trip over an asteroid trying to get to the other side. Running. Rushing. Something's stopping me. Up. I have to run up. Wait. It's a wall. Run up the wall. Through the wall. Move the wall. Find the elephant.

Stop. What's that sound? Glass. I'm knocking on the window. There's someone out there. They can help. Elevate the window.

"Sir? Or Madam? Would you help me save my elephant?"

Zombies. Or maybe just crazy. They won't help. Why won't they help? Perhaps I can sound the alarm and someone will come to my aid.

"Missing elephant!"

Those trees are alive. They'll help. Moving toward me. Angry. Dark. They'll hurt me, not help me. Sharp ends. Stab. Stab. No eyes. I have eyes. "Stop tree! Or I shall prune you."

Close the window. Safety. "Get away! Get away! Get away!" Slam.

Shiny everywhere. Cool. Clear. Shiny. Shiny. Water. Sharp water. All of it. I have to drink all of it.

Sharp. Cold. Sharp.

Quiet.

11

The Copper Bowl

"Bless me Father for I have sinned." *A creak from the kneeling bench.*

"How long since your last confession, my son?"

"2 years, Father."

"How have you sinned?"

"Father it is indeed a somewhat long and entailed matter." *A pause.*

"Take your time and speak openly. There is no rush."

"Father, two years ago I was in a position much like yourself. I was the priest of a small church in a non-descript village between Hastings and London. There were very few Anglicans in the town, and they went to a church a few miles away in the next village. Oddly enough we Catholics heavily outweighed them." *The sound of shifting cloth from the other side.*

"Permit me to interrupt you. You spoke in the past tense, meaning you are no longer with the church?"

"That is correct. A rather distressing incident occurred which I wish to relate to you so that I may seek absolution. My congregation was a small one, but the members were devoted to the humanitarian projects I sought to inject through the church. Nothing too radical you see, visiting shut ins, raising money for the local school, care packages to soldiers from the village who were abroad. My predecessor was somewhat elderly, and I am told he didn't like change. This seemed to have tried the patience of the village at times, so when I arrived and sought to make some minor adjustments, I was greeted with open arms. I was fresh out of the Seminary, and I wanted to make my own little mark. I suppose it was sinful and arrogant but I thought I might have been able to actually make a difference in the lives of the parishioners." *A pause.*

"Why have you stopped speaking my son?"

"What comes next is somewhat difficult. I had been there more than four months when this incident occurred and had performed just about every duty, except a baptism. As I said the village is small, and there weren't a lot of young married couples, so a birth was a very joyous affair. When my first opportunity arose, it was greeted with great excitement. The church was filled to capacity with relatives and well wishers. The parents were beaming, a very handsome couple. Annabella and Timothy. Before she had their baby, Annabella had worked as secretary to the local doctor, and Timothy taught the upper form at the school. They were devoted to one another and had the respect of everyone in town. I recall being invited to their home to discuss the proceedings, and while I was there I noted the modest, yet well maintained property. Timothy had a huge, long haired black and white cat that sat on his desk. After that first visit I returned on one or two occasions, and I always remember seeing that cat, sitting on the desk or looking out the window." *A pause and the sound of clearing one's throat.* "I apologize for the delay. The events are still somewhat difficult to recall."

"Perhaps it would help if you transitioned slowly. Tell me more about Annabella and Timothy."

"Well, Annabella was of average height for a woman, I suppose. Thin, and always neatly dressed, with her hair fixed. I believe the pregnancy was a healthy one, without complication. Timothy was tall and thin. It was my understanding that he was formerly quite athletic, but suffered an injury to his leg, resulting in a slight limp. On occasion he would carry a cane." *A sniff.* "Let me see, what else? They always had time to assist their neighbors, or to volunteer for church activities. Nothing of concern ever came to my ears which was uncommon of most of the population."

"Was your village inclined toward gossip?"

"More than I was accustomed to. But I should continue with the story. Timothy and Annabella were at the front of the church facing me with their backs to the well wishers in the pews. The baptismal font stood in front of them. It came up to about my waist and was constructed much like a table, out of cement. The bowl containing the holy water was copper and quite deep, as well as wide. I was facing the couple preparing to take the child, Bartholomew, so that I could dip his head into the holy water. The organ was playing, but I can't recall which hymn, it's blotted out of my memory. The congregation was full of smiles and excited faces, though no one looked happier than the young parents. Annabella handed baby Bartholomew to me. He was dressed in a crisp white christening gown and looked at me with curious blue eyes. I was nervous. It was my first baptism and such a big event for the parish that I harbored great concern over conducting it incorrectly. I recall the flashes of light emanating from cameras just as I took the baby. I opened my mouth to begin and that was when the unthinkable happened. I dropped the baby."

A sudden movement created by surprise. "You dropped him?"

"Yes. I don't know how it happened. I have lain awake for days at a time over the past two years attempting to understand how it could have occurred. I had Bartholomew in my hands holding him above the water and than something just happened. What I don't know, but the next thing I remembered was the sound of something splashing into the water and then I realized it was the baby. Gasps were heard and one or two lone chuckles, as if it were a staged farce. Timothy, Annabella, and I were too shocked to move at first. After a few seconds which felt like hours, the godfather, Harris, pushed Timothy aside and reached for Bartholomew. As if it were yesterday I recall him lifting the tiny form from the water. The christening gown was sodden and dripping like a jellyfish. There was blood in the water, as if someone had dropped a bit of food coloring into a glass. It slowly turned the clear water a sickening pink. At that moment I felt such a degree of powerlessness, unlike anything I had felt before."

"You did not act out of malice though. From what you have related to me, this was truly an accident." *A pause of some seconds.* "You remain silent. I understand this is very difficult. Do you wish to continue?"

"Yes Father. When I was able to tear my gaze away from the duel occurring in the water, I realized Harris had rushed out of the church, followed quickly by the village doctor and the parents. Many of the attendees likewise exited. I was left nearly alone in the church with a blood and holy water filled baptismal font. I'm not sure how long I actually stood there before I came to my senses and left the church."

"While this tragedy was indeed horrific, I have yet to see any wrong doing on your part."

"There is much more Father. I retreated to the vestry where I changed out of my baptismal robes and then proceeded to the doctor's surgery. I recall a few people milling about on the street, exchanging hushed words with one another. The majority of that activity stopped when I arrived and all eyes shifted to me. No one spoke to me, and I wasn't sure of whom I should ask information. Just as I was about to go into the surgery, Timothy emerged from the building. I implored him to forgive me for what I had done, and queried of his son." *A pause.*

"What happened to the baby?"

"Timothy told me he was dead. As I said the font was cement and it seemed he hit his head on the side before falling into the water. Timothy had a rather blank look on his face, and I braced myself, anticipating that he would lash out at me with his fists. He didn't. I wanted him to, but what he did instead was perhaps the worst. He simply said, 'It was an accident. Annabella and I understand. We forgive you.' It was at that moment that I felt sicker than I ever had before. I heard no sounds and everything around me was blurred except Timothy's face. At that moment discerning what was up and what was down was impossible. The sky could have been consumed by fire for all I could tell. Nearly speechless, another round of apologies exited my mouth, while the eyes of the village followed me back to the vicarage."

"Clearly Timothy understood there was no ill will on your part in relation to what transpired. His forgiveness, as you relate it, seemed genuine."

"I think it was. I never saw Annabella again, so I don't know if she shared his feelings. Upon returning to the vestry I removed the copper bowl from the font, suppressing bile and vomit in the process, and emptied the amalgamated fluid down the drain. This was followed by half an hour of overzealous scrubbing with scalding water and soap, which left my hands red and raw, though the pain was something of a blessing."

A pause.

"Take your time. Collect yourself and continue when you are able."

"No one came into the church that evening for late prayers. I alone occupied a pew, praying fervently for an answer which did not arrive. I realized what I had to do. I walked into the vestry and collected a knife from a drawer where tools and other things were kept. The clock struck twelve. Midnight. Turning off the lights caused magnitudes of moonlight to spill through the windows. Knife in hand I approached the baptismal font and removed the lid. With no hesitation, once across the left wrist and then with some difficulty another across the right wrist. The knife fell to the floor with a clatter. I dropped to my knees and held my wrists over the bowl so that the offering seeping forth could be collected." *Silence.*

"Yet you clearly didn't succeed in your attempt? Who found you?"

"From there it gets worse. Timothy found me. I'm told he couldn't sleep and wanted to talk with me. Talk! Not lash out at me. Not yell at me. He wanted to talk with me. I suppose he found me on the floor. I don't remember anything after I dropped to my knees. My next memory was of sitting in hospital in London."

"Suicide is a grievous sin. Had you been successful there is no doubt you would have been condemned to Hell for all eternity."

"Is that not what I deserved? I didn't know what else to do Father. What could be worse than destroying a whole village? Because that is what I did. By dropping that baby I killed something in each one of those people. For that I felt as though I had to die."

"What you did was an accident. There was no malice nor ill will contained within in your actions."

"It is difficult to agree with you Father."

"What have you done since that incident?"

"Well, I haven't set foot back in the village. There was no possible way I could face any of the people in that village again. I took a leave of absence of one year, after which I was assigned to another church, with a very able capable curate. He handles the baptismal arrangements."

"Has this new arrangement provided a fulfilling life for you?"

"I have learned to cope with my lot in life. I joined the priesthood not so much to spread the dogma of the church, but to help people. As I told you earlier I thought this would be a way for me to make the lives of people better." *A pause.* "In the end I may have done that, but I've also destroyed a life. I have trouble sleeping peacefully at night. I'm plagued by horrid nightmares where I'm covered in blood or am drowning in the ocean. However, I no longer recoil when I see a baby. I still wish to seek absolution for my sin."

The creak of the wooden seat. "You know as well as I that I can certainly assess a penance and absolve you of your sins, but you must also forgive yourself. Are you prepared to do that?"

A pause.

12

Manifesto

PART I

I've started smoking again. I shouldn't be, but it's so difficult not to while writing. Dropping my battered Moleskin notebook in that puddle last week didn't help either. The red ink looked like watered down blood spatters all over the edges of the pages. Not a great deal was lost, and truth be told I like the crinkled look and sound of the now dried sheets of paper. The water loosened the adhesive glue of both my Kucinich for President sticker and my "Leave the Mountains the Fuck Alone" sticker. Kucinich was so sodden it dropped back into the puddle. The second had begun to peel off so much that I slowly, with surgical precision, pulled it off the book, lest it simply read "Fuck Alone."

After the journal dried out, I spent a good ten minutes staring at the cover, attempting to ascertain whether or not the spots where the stickers had been were a shade lighter than the rest. There was no discernable difference and that disappointed me. To think I had made countless notes, observations, threats, and other musings in that book over the past two months, and yet, I hadn't imparted flakes of dead skin, or grim from my fingers onto the cover, in any noticeable quantity. Neither had the crumbs, grease, or spilled liquids from the table tops of the, at times noisy, at times quiet, bars and cafes I frequented, managed to penetrate the invisible dirt barrier which seemed to exist on the mid-sized, black collection of bound pages. I was certain to remove the folded up $50 bill that I kept in the back pocket for emergencies, so it could dry properly.

The smell of moldy money always turns my stomach. I suppose the aversion was a result of leaving wet laundry in the washing machine for a week, and then only taking it out to extract money from the pocket of my jeans. The smell was overpowering and I was forced to carry it with me until, in a fit of irritation, I spent $100 on tennis balls, just to get the horrible smell off my person.

I'm sitting in one of those aforementioned cafes now, a good two hours from my campus. The term café is used loosely around here. After all, a state who typically ranks 49th out of 50 in education, isn't bound to have the finest espresso or gourmet coffees. My espresso has been infused with too much water, because the carbuncular young woman behind the counter didn't tamp the grounds down tightly enough. By seating myself in a corner next to the window I can survey the entire room and the street in front from behind my aviator sunglasses. It's impossible to tell what this storefront originally housed, but now some rickety tables and chairs are strewn about. The tops are littered with bits of food and dried splashes of coffee. One might think a coke head had been camped out at the table next to mine, as there was a white substance scattered carelessly about. Of course it's only sugar. A sofa sits against the back wall. The fabric looks like something from That 70's Show, and one leg is missing, causing it to list backward on the left side. A small coffee table is directly in front of it with preciously two magazines. People and Time. The former of the two is dog eared, while the latter is pristine. An apt commentary of life in this area.

I'm the only person sitting in here right now. During my previous visits, it has been easy to notice that the peak times are between 8am and 10am, and noon and 1pm. Office workers, miners, and store clerks stop in during the first slot to fill up their cups and thermoses with cheap coffee that always smells like burnt dough. During the lunch hour the absence of the miners is obvious, but the other groupings come in to select from four meat infested sandwiches, and I do use the term meat loosely, or two watery soups. The place stays open until 5pm, but I've been the sole customer since 1:30, some two hours prior.

The third espresso is just as watery as the first two, thus explaining my lack of a flurried heart beat, or shaky hand. My noisy Moleskin is open, a red pen beside it, along with my copy of Rules for Radicals. Alinsky makes some good points, but I typically carry it to ensure people know where I stand. My afternoon has been spent looking for sentences to add to my personal manifesto.

A group of middle school students is slowly making their way down the street. I observe, attempting to look as non-predatory as possible.

Three guys and two girls. No backpacks, which I conclude means no homework. 50th in the nation, quite soon. I tilt my head down, as if to read, but my eyes continue to remain focused on the exterior world, safely so behind my glasses. Perhaps they can be characters in my fictional account of small town West Virginia. A group of middle school friends, uninterested in education, because its importance isn't properly expressed. Of course, one of them may become a doctor, or attorney, or even governor, but chances are they won't. They've passed without leaving behind any note worthy action or impression.

The shop attendant is on her cell phone, projecting her voice loudly at whomever is on the other end. It sounds as though date night is ruined. I return to Alinsky, after deciding another shot of espresso is out of the question.

***

I went to another protest today. Our own great, intellectually stunted junior United States Senator is leading the effort to draw back the EPA's ruling on MTR. A disappointingly small number of people showed up at his regional office. A few aging hippies with gray hair. Some scruffy college students, and a few fellow grad school hipsters. We didn't do much, other than wander about with signs carrying slogans like "Republican Joe" and "Shame on you Senator." I'd have opted for something a little more inflammatory, but I'm not really into the arts and crafts side of things.

One reporter showed up, from the local, weekly newspaper. She asked about three questions and then took her leave. We did manage to get one or two people who were passing by to promise to call or write to the Washington office in support of our cause. The placement of his office isn't ideal for protests, which was probably his Chief of Staff's idea. It was located in a mostly vacant office building at the edge of town. No shops, no restaurants, no apartment buildings or houses. A few cars did drive by, but they didn't stop.

After about three hours I decided to call it quits and walk back to my car. Most of the college students and the other grad students had already left. One of the older protesters, a man in his early 50's asked me if I had any "grass," to which I simply responded by rolling my eyes and handing him the sign I had been carrying.

***

It took me two hours to get home. I smoked a lot while I was in the car. My roommate doesn't like me to smoke in the apartment, and is constantly leaving me irritating notes to that affect. Notes, which I often contemplate shredding and putting in his food, when he isn't looking. I suppose everyone has to have one token Republican friend. It wouldn't be so bad if he idolized someone like Dick Lugar or Gerry Ford, politicians who may be conservative, but who will at least acknowledge that the other side is allowed to breath. Instead, his SUV, made in America of course, has a "Sarah!" bumper sticker, he blasts that dick Glenn Beck's television show, and he believes Barack Obama was born and raised in another country, where he most likely received extensive training in terrorism.

We were at the same prep school together. Not exactly best mates, but friends none the less. I think he may actually have been my lab partner in freshmen biology. We lost contact while at college. He went to WVU, I fled to the University of Rhode Island. It was only through the magic of Facebook, that we ended up being roommates. I decided to return to West Virginia for graduate school, moved close to the campus and posted the fact that I needed a roommate as my status. A day letter a message from my former lab partner awaited me, informing me that he was trying for a MBA at the same school, and here we are.

***

I was two blocks from my apartment, finishing another ciga-rette. My headlights caught a cat as it darted across the street. The building used to be a gigantic house, but is now divided into five apartments. My pal and I have the third floor. It was advertised as a three bedroom apartment, but I knew I needed one of those rooms for my books. There's only one bathroom, but we have our own kitchen and a big sitting room. Most of my time there is spent in my bedroom or with the books. An ex-girlfriend used to say I had developed prison pallor from spending so much time holed up in there. That's one reason why I've taken to getting in the car and driving out to one of the dinky little counties and setting up shop for a few days.

The oval advertising only the first name, with a cheerleaderish, red exclamation mark afterwards was visible as I pulled into one of three parking spots with signs with a black "5" in front of them. The third spot housed another American bred car, this one emblazoned with a myriad of right leaning slogans, including "Don't blame me, I voted for the only American in the race." Guests. Republican guests. Decisions, decisions. Bar? Hotel? Friend's house? Parents' home? Not that desperate yet. Bar.

I decided to walk, so as not to worry about leaving my car on the street, due to a projected inability to drive resulting from an antici-pated over consumption of beer. There is a small bar, or "pub" as the owners opted to call it, about four blocks from the apartment. It is frequented by artsy college and grad students, thus it yielded very little in my efforts to discover the real West Virginia. On the up-side, it's near by, and serves lots of locally brewed beer. I emp-tied my backpack of everything except my journal, a copy of Can

God and Caesar Co-Exist?, my red pen, wallet, and phone. Father Drinan was a pretty awesome guy, and I'm finding a ton of stuff to use in my own writing.

The walk to the bar was quiet, and only took a few minutes. 730 on a Wednesday evening wasn't a busy time for any of the places I passed. A car drove by every so often, and at least one truck. At times I find it interesting to hypothesize where the people in the automobiles are going, where they've been, who they are. A guy about my age passed me, bag over his shoulder, a plastic bag presumably carrying take out food in his left hand. Probably just left class. Could be a grad student, probably an undergraduate, though. It's difficult for me to tell sometimes, because I'm younger than most of the other graduate students. He might be on his way back to his apartment after classes. The shoulder bag looked like it was full of books. Literature, maybe. Or history. He'll probably spend the rest of the night studying, managing to spill lo mien noodles, or tomato sauce on his notes.

I had arrived. The sign read "Mel's." From the outside, it looked a bit like a dive. Small brick place, sandwiched in between two other buildings. They served food, and thereby somehow were permitted to have a large plate glass window in the front, allowing passersby to look in. I never completely understood what the dividing line was between these places. Why are some allowed to have windows, while others have to board them up? Presumably so small children don't see their parents inside getting drunk and projectile vomiting all over some poor fellow drunk's pants. The three cement steps leading inside were cracked, and it was typically advisable to hold onto the metal railing, which looked like a series of plumbing pipes that someone welded together to avoid tripping on the uneven pavement. The urban legends about the place reveal that it was supposedly a bar for locals until about six years ago when a group of history students started hanging out inside. Pretty soon the town residents couldn't find sufficient table or bar space, due to the throngs of students who showed up. The cheap commercial beer was replaced with imported selections and locally brewed varieties, an odd juxtaposition. Youth centered bands started playing on Friday nights. Pretty soon, the place became a hangout for the local grad school students, too.

It was quiet, even for a Wednesday night. I saw one of my archnemeses sitting at a round, wooden table near the bar. I say archnemesis, but I suppose a qualification is in order. It isn't that we're really even acquainted. He's just one of those people who happens to be in a class I have, who sometimes passes me on campus, and who a professor might reference in a conversation. There was a mutual dislike between us, though we'd only spoken on a few rare occasions, and none of those yielded any sort of disagreement, or agreement for that matter. He had a lot of hair, not that it was long, just thick, and typically wore shirts with horizontal stripes. A fellow graduate school student who was pursuing studies in English, a play of his had been performed on campus last semester. To say that gratuitous violence was a cornerstone would be an understatement. On top of that, he's a Republican who masquerades as a holier than thou moderate. I've never really understood how advanced education leads to conservatism, unless one has something to gain from it. Letting that thought hang, I dumped my bag on the table, and sauntered over to the bar.

Mel's features quite a robust selection of locally brewed beers, including one called Red Tick Beer. It is sold by a couple of twenty something locals, and the name was acquired from an episode of The Simpsons. I remain unsure as to how they avoided some sort of copyright infringement. It's okay, but I prefer Heineken, even though I want to support local merchants. What can you do, though? They also sell exception French fries, made with peanut oil, rather than lard. After procuring a basket of the aforementioned potatoes, and a cold, green bottle, I returned to my table, which just happened to face my stripey friend.

He was scribbling away in a spiral notebook. Another play? Perhaps this one will feature someone being decapitated with a chainsaw, rather than dismembered with an axe. Ignoring him was better than wasting time pondering what he was actually doing. I turned to my own work, and began a formulation, using Father Drinan's ideas, of permitting religious observation without any infringement upon the secular state. Separation of church and state seemed a little far a field for a simple manifesto about a green, youth centered West Virginia, but when your local town council meetings still start with a prayer, it has to be addressed. Father Drinan served faithfully in Congress for several terms and never let his enormous faith interfere with his academically sound interpretation of the fundamental rule of law in the United States. While he personally opposed abortion, he also understood that Roe v. Wade is considered settled law. I tend to automatically dismiss any candidate who makes the right to choose a cornerstone of any political campaign.

Chapters from "It's Just a Life," an unfinished novel

13

Just Another Day

"Jesus Fucking Christ!" A bottle flew past my head and smashed into the wall. I glanced to my left and saw Ric deliver a hard right to the face of one of the attackers. I picked up a pool cue and drove it into the gut of the guy rushing toward me. He sucked in a breath and doubled over. Josh was on my right. He socked a guy in the face hard enough that his lip split and sent drops of blood spraying as his head snapped to the side. Another one was advancing toward me, but I introduced his stomach to the sole of my sneaker.

We brawled with them for a few more minutes, until they finally realized we had the advantage and ran out through the fire exit. Luckily we had been the only people in the pool room. Unluckily though Joe had heard the ruckus and appeared at the doorway with a baseball bat.

"What have I told you damn kids about coming in here and starting fights?"

Ric picked up a pool cue that was on the floor and put it back on the wall. "They started it. Those idiots know this is our turf. They came here to start trouble." Ric was a year older than me, 17. But he was the shortest one of us, probably about 5'7". He was skinny, but surprisingly strong for someone his size. His black hair was combed straight up into a 5" Mohawk, which made him look taller than me.

"I don't got no care for who started what. You'd better clean up this mess, or I'll knock all your heads in."

He stood there for a moment or so, and watched us as we started to clean up broken glass and put tables right side up again. Satisfied that we were earnest, he went back into the bar. As you can probably guess this isn't the first time Joe's met us at the doorway with a baseball bat after we kicked some rival ass. In fact, I can't even remember how many times he's threatened to knock our heads in. I got a broom out of the small supply closet which was between the bar and the pool room and swept up all of the broken glass.

"Why do you think those guys came here tonight?" Josh asked.

He was examining his hand. The skin on his knuckles looked like someone had taken red paint and carelessly dropped it haphazardly onto the skin. One word describes Josh, awkward. He's really tall, about 6'3" and athletically built, but pretty clumsy. It's like he hasn't grown into his body yet. He's always tripping over stuff, or running into something. He's the same age as Ric, but with a more conventional haircut. "We ain't had a beef with Jack and his gang in weeks."

"That might be my fault," Ric said. His right eye had begun to turn purple.

Josh and I stopped what we were doing and looked at him.

"You see, Jack may have caught me in what you might call a compromising situation with his girl."

It figures. Ric has trouble keeping his pants zipped up, which has led to several rough scrapes for us. Luckily this one ended a little better than the time Ric hit on some college girl and we ended up being chased by half of their football team.

Since the pool room appeared to be back in order we decided to split for the night. Josh led the way out of the fire exit in order to escape another series of threats from Joe. As we rounded the side of the building I glanced up at the sign which was on the front: "Joe's Luxury Pool Hall and Bar". It had red neon tubes that flashed. I never was sure what made it luxurious. It looked like an ordinary bar on the inside. The outside was just a brick building, next to another brick building which sold art supplies and made custom frames. There were beer bottle green windows on Joe's building. There were really high up though. If Josh jumped he could just see inside. Of course I'm no expert when it comes to ranking bars. This is the only one I've been in, being only 16. Joe has always looked the other way when neighborhood kids went in. He's only served us alcohol when we're still hanging around at closing and everyone else has gone.

You're probably wondering why the police have never busted him? Well, around my neighborhood we never see the police unless someone calls them, and even then it's wishful thinking. We don't really have much crime. I can't remember anyone ever being murdered. Just the normal stuff: fights; cars stolen and then returned with dents and no gas; broken windows; public drunkenness. I do remember this one time when I was about 13, a kid my brother hung around with got knifed because he owed some pusher $100. Most of us aren't stupid enough to become dope heads just delinquents.

***

We were walking past some houses. They were small, but mostly well kept.

The driveways usually only had one car, which wasn't that new and might have some paint chipping off or something. The houses were sometimes in need of fresh paint. But it wasn't like every house had busted out windows and people passed out on the lawns. The majority of the people who worked in the factories lived here. I guess you'd call them lower middle class. (Sounds like what my history teacher would say). I thought about my Dad. He had been a foreman in one of them. He died 5 years ago. My Mom's one of the only people around here who went to anything after High School.

She's a nurse at the hospital. But with three kids and a house, we don't have much extra money.

I stopped and looked at one of the houses. The windows were boarded up and had graffiti painted all over. If I believe it, Julie is really easy and GJH and NAC love one another. Julie was in red and the lovebirds were painted in black. The grass hadn't been mowed in months. With the dim light from the street lamps, I could barely make out a cat which sat on the porch watching us with a snotty stare. Josh and Ric were standing next to me.

"Do you think that cat lives there?" Josh asked.

"Probably," Ric replied. "It doesn't look rich enough to own the house, it probably rents." He gave one of his loud explosive laughs at his own joke.

Josh swore at him and gave him a hard shove. Yet Ric continued to laugh as he stumbled backwards.

Sometimes it seems like Josh doesn't have a lot of common sense. He'll ask questions and then realize the answer is obvious, or that he just has things backwards in his mind. While I'm the only one of the three of us who gets A's, Josh does all right in school. Ric on the other hand is lucky to pass. He's probably as smart or smarter than me, but he never does his homework. He can sit in class and absorb everything the teacher says like a sponge, and spit it back onto the tests, which is only good for C's and D's if you don't turn anything else in.

We continued our walk, not really going in one particular direction. It was probably close to 11pm, but I couldn't be sure. None of us wear watches. They break too easily. I stopped to zip up my jacket. It was getting colder already, and the leaves had only begun to change. "Where are we going?"

"You want to go to the Strip?"

I looked at Josh and we both shook our heads. "No car."

"We could swipe one," Ric suggested. He was shuffling from one foot to the other.

"It's too late to start something like that," I replied.

I've heard most towns have something like the Strip. It's just a line of restaurants, stores and drive-in theaters. It's always loud, always busy and always has some fun to offer. There are cars racing around, kids yelling, and general mischief. It's our favorite place to hang out. For some reason the powers that be have kept really good care of it. The road doesn't have any potholes or anything like that. There isn't garbage all over the ground and all of the businesses are well kept. I guess the city council or whatever realizes it makes a lot of money for the area. Even some of the kids who live in the small towns out in the country bring their trucks here every now and then. During the day a bunch of old women usually take the bus or drive their giant cars down here and go shopping. In the afternoon there are mothers going to the grocery store and stuff. But after dark is when all of the kids come out and it's really a hot place to be.

The bitch of the thing is that none of has a car. My mom does, but she rarely lets me use it. Ric's Dad has a truck, but he's not allowed near it. (That's a long story). Josh has managed to wrangle his parents' car away from them on a few occasions. None of us had much luck during the week, which usually led us to swipe one when we really needed it.

We kept wandering around for a while and finally ended up in a small park. It was empty. Ric slumped down into an old bench. I sat on the back of it and rested my feet on the seat. Josh remained standing and lit a cigarette. He took a long draw and then passed it around to the rest of us.

Cigarettes were a necessity for us, yet a constant drain on what little money we had. Ric and I had perfected stealing them from the closest drug store. Josh wasn't quite as capable. He usually nearly got caught or became too freaked out to actually make it out of the building with them. We had to be careful too. If they ever did an inventory or something and found out cigarettes always went missing when we were in the store, I doubt they would look the other way when we actually came in to purchase them legally, even though we aren't 18.

I took a last drag from the cigarette and handed it back to Josh so he could finish. We continued to sit in silence until Ric spoke.

"Are we just going to sit here all night?"

I stood up and jumped off the bench. "Well what do you want to do? We have no car, hardly any money, and stuff's gonna start closing soon."

"I might as well have stayed home and done my homework."

Josh dropped the cigarette butt he was holding. "Well we did get to fight a little bit. That amounts to something."

***

You're probably wondering why a bunch of teenagers are wondering around that late at night. (Plus it was a school night). It's just how it is in our neighborhood. My Mom loves it when I'm home early, and I'm sure she worries when I'm out late, but half the time she has to work night shifts at the hospital, so she's found it easier to give me free reign and hope for the best. Josh has to sneak out most of the time. I swear his parents must know he leaves and comes back through the window. (He probably falls and knocks stuff over every time). I think it's one of those things, where if they don't see it, they pretend they don't know. Ric on the other hand pretty much comes and goes as he pleases. His father works 14 hour days and goes home to eat and then sleeps, so he almost never knows what's going on. His mother is pretty much drunk most of the time and doesn't care.

We left the park and wandered around for a little while longer. Nothing interesting appeared to be happening, so we split off and went home. I was about a block from my house when I saw someone weaving around on the sidewalk ahead of me. He continued to move forward and walked under one of the few street lamps with a bulb in it. I realized it was Dave, a kid who lived a few houses away from me. He was carrying a brown bag that had a bottle inside of it. He seemed pretty wrecked. He was a year older than me, and we didn't really hang around together, but we knew each other pretty well I guess. He must have just realized who I was, because he stopped.

"Will, man, how's it goin?" He was slurring a good bit and looked pretty wobbly on his feet. I noticed he had a newspaper clutched in his other hand. He read at least one, sometimes two or three newspapers a day, depending upon how many he could swipe.

"I'm cool, Dave. You heading home?"

"Yeah, man. Got school tomorrow."

"You're turned around," I said. "You're going in the wrong direction. Here, follow me."

"Awesome man, I really appreciate this." He brushed his shaggy hair out of his eyes and looked at me. "You know Walt's going to loose? He should win, but he's not." He held up the newspaper, and then I realized what he meant.

"Yeah, well I don't think it's going to help or hurt either of us."

He put the bottle in the pocket of his jacket and slung his arm around my shoulders. He began to speak in a very conspiratorially manner. "That's where you're wrong." His breath reeked of alcohol. It made me want some. I considered asking him for the bottle, but decided not to.

"Walt would be a fuckin' good President." He held up the front page of the paper so I could see the headline. *Reagan Widens Lead with Two Months To Go.* "Gerry ain't too bad lookin' either."

"She's old enough to be your mom."

"So what, man?" He still had his arm around my neck, and was resting part of his weight on my shoulders. It made me wonder if this was his first bottle of the evening. He started fumbling in his pocket and pulled the bottle out. He took a drink and held it in front of me. "You want some?"

"I guess." I took the bottle and downed a mouthful. Gin. The burn down the back of my throat felt good. I reluctantly passed the bottle back to him.

We were approaching my house, but I thought it might be a good idea for me to actually walk him to his, so he didn't end up asleep in a ditch 10 miles away. I could tell the T.V. was on in my house. Mom was working a night shift and my kid brothers probably didn't expect me to be home so soon. They were supposed to be in bed. I usually made a big show of yelling at them if they weren't in bed when I got home and Mom was out. I don't know why I do it, especially since the 14 year old is pretty big for his age and in a couple of years will probably be able to kick my ass if I'm not careful.

Dave lived 4 houses down. His house was dark and his parents' car wasn't in the driveway.

"Where are your parents?"

"Oh, they're away for two days, man. Visiting my aunt. She just had a kid." He caught his foot on something and stumbled a little bit.

I began to wonder if he would stay put if I took him to his house, or leave again.

"Why don't you stay at my house tonight?"

He pushed the hair out of his eyes again and looked at me. "Dude, that's like the nicest thing anyone has done for me in a long time." He patted me hard on the back.

I steered him back towards my house and up the creaky steps of the porch. I opened the squeaky screen door and tried to open the front door while balancing Dave.

The T.V. was off, but I could hear footsteps running upstairs. They must have heard me come up the porch.

"Yeah, you'd better get your asses into bed, or I'll bust your lips."

"Stop trying to be like Ron, man," Dave said. "I bet Walt doesn't talk to his parents like that."

"I was yelling at my brothers." I guided him upstairs and into my room. I kept a couple of old sleeping bags in my closet in case Ric or Josh slept over. I pulled one out and dropped it on the floor.

Dave took his jacket, shoes and jeans off and clumsily climbed into the sleeping bag. I went to the bathroom, and when I came back he had started singing to himself.

"Could you not do that? I have school tomorrow morning."

He didn't respond, but shut up a few seconds later. I undressed and laid down in my bed. Just another day.

14

Just a Car

The Strip is really blazing tonight. A bunch of sports cars just raced by the place where we're parked. A pack of 13 or 14 year olds are spraying one another with that silly string stuff they sell at toy stores, in the next parking lot. No cops yet. I see a bunch of kids trying to cram themselves into a telephone booth across the road. I didn't think people did that anymore. They must have seen it on an episode of Happy Days or something. Fridays and Saturdays are always the busiest nights for the places here. Kids from all over the city come here every night, but the weekends see a larger number. It's really the only place where rich kids, middle class kids, black kids, white kids, poor kids, good kids, and bad kids all come together. There are sports cars parked next to ancient wrecks. Kids wearing designer clothes walk into the same movie theater as those wearing clothing their siblings had out grown. The best part is they don't outright hate one another either. Most of the poorer kids are jealous of the rich kids of course, but they don't have fights over it. Of course sometimes they do have fights just for the sake of fighting, but not because they're different or anything. Sometimes you'll see a guy and his girlfriend come out of a store with like six bags in their hands and talk with some kid with one small bag, who clearly isn't as well off. I guess it's sort of like the country as a whole. There are people of all kinds of backgrounds.

There are always lots of blinking neon lights, music blaring out of drive in restaurants, horns blowing, shouting and engines revving. All sorts of fast food restaurants and diners are stuck between movie theaters and stores. All of the famous names are there, Dairy Queen, McDonalds, Wendy's, Sonic's. Some of the restaurants are eat in only, others have drive-thrus, and some still have a car-hop system. There are still two drive in theaters left, which are more popular than the regular theaters, but they don't have a lot of space. Most of the places to eat stay open until midnight during the week, and one or two on the weekends. The theaters do the same thing. Not many stores are open past ten, with a few exceptions. Most of the gas stations stay open later. There are also some specialty shops who maintain different hours. This book store that's near one of the drive in theaters stays open until midnight. I don't know why. I've never been in it, but every time I go by it's dead inside. Even though things eventually close there's always something to do, not matter what time it is.

Most of the groups of kids have their favorite places to go. Josh, Ric, and I usually get there around seven and eat at one of the hamburger drive ins, if we have the money. After that a trip to the drug store for cigarettes is usually in order. Again, if we have the money, one of us will usually buy a couple of packs while the others look at the magazines or hang around in front. If we don't have any money, Ric or I will go in alone and swipe a couple of packs when no one is looking. Next we usually head over to one of the drive in theaters, if they aren't full. Luckily we only need to pay for one person, while the other two hide in the trunk. I still wonder why the people who work there haven't caught onto to that yet. Maybe they just don't care. After the movie were generally try to pick up some girls, or meet up with some other kids we know. Once and a while they'll be a fight or a drag race or something.

The cops make a few sweeps up and down each night, but you can usually find them parked at a restaurant. But I have seen them break up quite a few kick ass fights and a couple of drag races.

All of this sounds like a lot of fun right? I mean what could be better than eating a bunch of fast food, sneaking into a movie and watching a bunch of little kids shoot colored string at one another? Well, we are always faced with one problem when it comes to planning a night on the Strip. One simple thing. Nothing fancy. Just a car. My mom has only let me borrow her car three or four times. Josh usually has a lot more luck, but tonight his parents had decided to go out. That left Ric's father's truck, which really isn't an option. We wouldn't be able to hide to get into the theater for one, and it wasn't exactly the best vehicle for picking up girls.

Right after school, we headed over to my house, where I got the bad news from my Mom.

"I have to pick up an extra shift tonight."

"I was hoping I could borrow the car. Can I take you to work and then pick you up when your shift is over?"

"No. The last time we tried that you didn't wake up on time and I had to take a taxi home. I don't want to pay for that again. Why don't you three stay in for the night. You know how I worry about you being out at all hours."

"I'll be fine, Mom."

We trooped up to my room and came up with zero possible solutions. We'd managed to save up a little money, so we really wanted to go out tonight, instead of hoping we could hang on to it by next weekend. Mom gives me a little each week, and Josh works one evening a week. Ric almost always comes up with more than both of us combined, usually from hustling pool, knocking around some younger kids, or picking a few pockets.

Finally Ric had a suggestion, "Why don't we just swipe one?"

"One what?"

"He means a car," I said.

I think this suggestion made Josh uncomfortable. "I don't know about that. We haven't tried anything like that in a couple of years since we got caught."

He was referring to a fuckin' scary run-in we almost had with not only the police, but also Heaven about two years ago. (Or possibly Hell). They were 15, and I was 14. We had ripped off cars before, but had just driven them around a few blocks or so in the middle of the night and then returned them. No big deal. In fact it happens a lot around here. This time, Ric thought it would be wicked if we went over to some of the higher end neighborhoods and swipe some really cool looking car. We found this huge house with like 4 cars parked in the front. I remember a Jaguar and a Cadillac. There was also some kind of sports car, but we ignored that because there were 3 of us, and not enough room. I don't remember what the other car was. Somehow Ric knew how to hotwire a car, so he broke the window on the passenger side of the Jaguar and unlocked it. Josh and I kept watch while he fooled with the wires. The house was totally dark and it must have been at least half past midnight. Just when he informed us he almost had the connection ready, a car pulled into the driveway. I don't know how we missed it. The headlights caught us and we all froze, Josh and I standing on either side of it, and Ric partially on the floor of the car under the steering wheel, and partially on the pavement of the driveway. The next thing I knew, a bunch of big, mean-looking guys had surrounded us. Like I said, this was two years ago, we were all smaller, and didn't know how to fight as well. I thought for sure I was going to die right there.

"What are you punks doing?" a brown haired guy in a Varsity Jacket asked. I could smell alcohol.

Josh and I were too afraid to say anything, but of course Ric was his usually smart ass self. "Well, gentlemen, you see we were just passing along and saw some street toughs attempting to break into this automobile. Personally, I think they may have been from the wrong side of the tracks. We chased them off, and then were just checking the damage. When you showed up, I was just about to go knock on the door and let the owners now what happened."

"Sure you were," the guy replied. "Well, my Dad owns the car that *you* broke into. What do you think guys? Should we call the police, or handle it ourselves?"

They had shut off the headlights of the car when they surrounded us. There was some light from the street lamps, and I think I counted six of them in a circle around us. I didn't give much for our odds.

"I think we ought to teach them to keep their filthy hands off other peoples' stuff," this came from black haired guy who looked like his nose had been broken at some point in his life.

Just when I thought I was about to get my face smashed in, several lights flickered on around the house and a voice was calling from the front porch. "What's going on out there?"

Everyone looked toward the porch and Ric yelled, "Run!"

The three of us blasted forward with our shoulders down. We managed to catch them off guard and run down the driveway. We didn't stop running until we were about 10 blocks away. All of us ducked into an alley to catch our breath. I listened and couldn't hear any footsteps.

"They must have decided to leave us alone," Josh said. He pulled a pack of cigarettes out of his pocket and passed it around along with a lighter. "That was a really bad idea." He balled up his fist and gave Ric a hard punch to the back.

Ric lurched forward and turned. "Don't blame it on me. How was I supposed to know anyone would show up." He kneeled down and rested his back against the wall of a brick building.

We all waited for a few minutes, smoking in silence and then walked back to our neighborhood and our homes.

*****

"So what are we going to do?" I asked.

"Just leave it to me," Ric said. "I'll meet the two of you back here at seven."

Although we were slightly skeptical, Josh and I agreed that we would leave it to him. Josh came back to my house almost right at seven. My Mom had left at six, with her car. Just a few minutes past seven Ric showed up driving an old dark blue Mercury. It wasn't in bad shape, just old.

"Where did you get it?" Josh asked.

"Well, I kept knocking on doors until someone lent it to me."

I walked around to the passenger side and got in, "Who lent it to you?"

"Oh, just a friend of the family."

Josh and I exchanged looks, we both realized he probably stole it. But I didn't care, we could take it back once we were finished.

So that brings us back to the present. Ric pulled into a place we always ate called Flame Burger. The sign had a hamburger surrounded by flames on it. I think it's supposed to mean they cook everything over open flames, but I'm not sure if I believe it. The food wasn't bad, and it wasn't as popular as some of the other places, so it was usually fairly easy to park. It was one of those drive in restaurants, where you pull in to these little spaces with menus on boards next to you. Then a waitress comes out and takes your order. They have a small place inside to eat, but that was usually where all of the adults went. Madonna was blaring out of the speakers. I don't like her, and I doubt if she'll last long. There were quite a few other cars, but no one we really knew that well. A few people I recognized were milling around, but no one I was close with.

We were unlucky enough to get one of the ugly waitresses. She took her time getting to us and then sort of shouted out "What do you want?" She was chewing gum really loudly too. We all ordered hamburgers, fries and cokes. It didn't take long for them to arrive and we ate leisurely. The side of the parking lot we were on faced the Strip and we watched the cars speed by. After I finished eating, I lit a cigarette and tried to make the smoke into rings. I'm not very good at that.

"Give me one," Ric said.

I handed him my pack and pretended not to notice that he took two, putting one in his pocket and the other in his mouth. He pushed the cigarette lighter in and waited for it to pop out.

A car pulled in next to us and I realized Dave was in it. He saw me and spoke, "Hey, Will man. How's it going?"

"I'm doing fine."

"Thanks again for helping me out last week. I might have wound up in the dump or something."

I looked to see who he was with. There was a guy I didn't recognize in the driver's seat, next to Dave. Steve and his girlfriend were in the backseat. Steve was a senior at our school. He was one of the few who was actually going to be able to go to college. I think he had the highest GPA in the whole class. People were always asking him for help in science or math. He won a bunch of academic awards all the time. His parents probably couldn't afford to send him to college, but he worked really hard and had received a scholarship to the State University. I'm not sure what he's going to study. His girlfriend was really good looking. I wonder what she's going to do when he's gone?

"Hey, let's go to the drive in theater, I heard they're playing a really good one," Josh suggested. "Something about some space alien that eats people's brains."

"That sounds like every movie they've ever played," Ric said.

The waitress eventually came back to us and we paid and drove out. Ric wasn't a very careful driver, and we nearly got the middle of the car smashed in when he pulled out into incoming traffic.

"Shit, would you be more careful." I didn't want to die tonight. There were a few more things I wanted to experience in life before I chucked it all in.

"Oh lighten up. I've been driving longer than either of you."

We pulled into the parking lot of a grocery store, which was getting ready to close for the evening. Josh and I got out of the car and walked around to the back. Luckily this one had a large trunk. My Mom's car isn't that big, and Josh care barely fold himself into the trunk and still leave any room for Ric. Josh got in first and then I got in.

"Will, move over. I think there's a tire iron in my back."

"I can't move over any more, I'm up against the side. Just sit still, we'll be there in a few minutes." I could feel the motion of the car as Ric pulled out into traffic.

"I think maybe we should just pay for the three of us the next time," Josh said.

"Why? That's expensive."

"I'm not all that comfortable with sitting this close to you in such a small space. It's kind of fruity."

"Hell, we're practically brothers. And believe it or not the height of my sexual fantasies doesn't involve being stuck in the trunk of an old car with you. Now if you were about a foot shorter, a woman, and had a different face and body, it might be another story."

The car stopped and I could hear the ticket salesman ask Ric if he was the only one in the car. "Of course I am. Do I look like the type of person who would try to sneak someone into the drive in theater?"

I didn't hear a response from the seller, but felt the car lurch forward. We waited until it had stopped again and then I opened the trunk and climbed out. Josh followed me and we got into the car. No one paid much attention to us, in fact there were several other car trunks opening with people climbing out. We had about ten minutes before the show began. "Do either of you want a soda?"

They both said yes and I went to the snack counter. While I was waiting in line I noticed a really cute girl from my school. She had already ordered and was waiting for her food. I told the attendant what I wanted and stepped to the side. Right next to her. "How's it going?"

She glanced at me, "Fine."

"You're in my Science class aren't you?"

"There are lots of people in my Science class, I can't be expected to remember all of them."

I'm not sure I like her attitude, but sometimes I've found you have to be persistent. "Take my word for it, I'm pretty sure you are."

"Come on back to mine. I leaned against the counter and looked at her as the attendant put my order down. "I'm told I'm a pretty good kisser."

She jerked her head toward me. "Well in that case." She took one of the sodas in my hand and poured it over my head. "My original answer still applies."

Luckily no one was paying much attention, or I would have been really embarrassed. She had turned and walked away. I carried the two remaining sodas back to the car and handed them through the window. I then took my jacket off and used it to dry my hair. I threw it into the back seat and then got in.

Ric glanced into the mirror and must have seen my wet hair. "It isn't raining is it?"

I grunted and lit a cigarette.

Top 10 Lists

15

...Reasons Fall is the Best Season

1.) Halloween

2.) Sweater weather

3.) Dry corn in fields

4.) Deluge of mystery novels

5.) New episodes of Judge Judy

6.) Nostalgia for high school in fall (yes, this counts)

7.) Re-reading *The Hardy Boys Ghost Stories*

8.) General elections

9.) A new *Almanac of American Politics* (only in odd years)

10.) Fewer snakes

16

...American Politicians

1.) Representative Shirley Chisholm of New York

2.) Senator Margaret Chase Smith of Maine

3.) President Franklin D. Roosevelt of New York

4.) Secretary Hillary Rodham Clinton of New York

5.) Representative Barbara Lee of California

6.) Governor Lincoln Chafee of Rhode Island

7.) Senator Jay Rockefeller of West Virginia

8.) Mayor John Lindsay of New York

9.) Senator Maria Cantwell of Washington

10.) Vice-President Hubert H. Humphrey, Jr. of Minnesota

17

...James Franco Projects

1.) *A California Childhood*

2.) *Esquire* interview conducted by Dave Franco

3.) *Spider-Man 3*

4.) *Palo Alto* (book or film)

5.) *Freaks and Geeks*

6.) *Directing Herbert White*

7.) *Child of God*

8.) *As I Lay Dying*

9.) My James Franco sweatshirt

10.) *James Dean*

18

...Comic Book Characters

1.) Archie Andrews

2.) Iceman

3.) Jughead Jones

4.) Spider-Woman (Jessica Drew)

5.) Scarecrow

6.) Thor

7.) Scarlet Witch

8.) Hotdog (Jughead's dog)

9.) Firestar

10.) Cloak & Dagger (always a pair)

19

...Non-Cardinal Sins

1.) Ending a sentence with "at" :-) (The emoji saves me.)

2.) Walking into a store and not buying something because it can be "ordered online"

3.) Failing to acknowledge the brilliance of James Franco's literary voice.

4.) Having sweatpants in one's "going to town" wardrobe.

5.) Not voting for any reason other than dire illness.

6.) The *Gilligan's Island* theme version that fails to list the Professor and Mary Anne, but rather says "and the rest."

7.) The wearing of jeans under judicial, academic, choir, or ecumenical robes.

8.) Unnecessary abbrs. (That one was necessary.)

9.) No skateboarding signs in perpetually empty parking lots. (That's for the 19 year old slacker me.)

10.) Incomplete top 10 lists.